JACK AND THE BEANSTALK

Jack and the Beanstalk

Retold by
Scudder Smith

Illustrated by
Felipe López Salán

Purple Bear Books
New York

ONCE UPON A TIME there was a boy named Jack who lived in a cottage in the country with his widowed mother. Jack's mother was not strong enough to work, and as the years passed, the two of them grew poorer and poorer until the only thing they had left was their milk cow.

Finally the day came when Jack's mother said sadly, "Jack, I'm afraid we must sell our cow to get money to buy food."

"All right, Mother," said Jack. "I'll take it to the market in town and make a fine bargain for us." And with that, Jack set off with the cow.

On the way to town, Jack saw a strange woman sitting at the side of the road.

"Come here, boy!" she said. "I have a wonderful deal for you. These five magic beans will bring you great fortune. I'll give them to you in exchange for your cow."

Jack thought for a while and then agreed. He couldn't wait to tell his mother about the fine bargain he had made.

When Jack got home, he gave the five magic beans to his mother.

"You fool!" she cried. "We need money to buy food! Our cow is gone and what is there to show for it?" Angrily, she threw the beans out the window. That night, Jack and his mother went to bed hungry.

The next morning, Jack and his mother woke to an amazing sight. Overnight, the beans had grown into a gigantic beanstalk that stretched high into the sky. Jack was stunned, but he was also curious. "I wonder what is at the top of the beanstalk," he said. "I think I'll go and find out."

So Jack climbed the beanstalk, right to the top. There among the clouds stood a huge castle. Jack hurried along the path to the castle door.

"What an enormous door!" he exclaimed. "I wonder who could live here." Jack knocked, but no one answered. Finding the door unlocked, he pushed it open and stepped inside.

"What are you doing here?" thundered a giant woman.

"I was hoping to find some milk," Jack replied. "I'm sorry if I disturbed you."

Hearing this, the woman became a bit more kindly. She bent down and said, "Come then, child. I will get you some milk. But drink it quickly. You must leave before my husband returns. He eats little ones like you."

Jack shivered with fear.

Suddenly a door slammed.

"Hurry!" whispered the giant woman. "Hide in the oven!"

Then a booming voice called out, "Fee-fi-fo-fum! I smell the blood of a little one!"

"A little one?" stammered his wife. "Of course not. You must be hungry. Sit down and I will make you some dinner."

Jack cowered in the oven and didn't dare make a sound.

After the giant had finished his dinner he took out a treasure chest filled with gold coins which he spread on the table to count. But before long, the giant fell fast asleep, snoring loudly.

Jack crept out of the oven, filled his pockets with gold coins, raced away from the castle, and quickly climbed down the beanstalk.

When Jack showed his mother the gold coins, she hugged him and cried with joy.

"See! The beans did bring us great fortune after all!" said Jack.

After that, Jack and his mother had plenty of money for food, and they lived quite happily for quite a while. But finally they spent the last gold coin.

"Don't worry, Mother," said Jack bravely. "I'll climb the beanstalk again and bring back some more of the giant's gold."

So once again Jack climbed the beanstalk high up above the clouds. He sneaked into the castle and hid in the oven.

"Fee-fi-fo-fum! I smell the blood of a little one!" boomed the giant, sniffing the air.

"A little one? Nonsense!" said his wife. "You must be hungry. Sit down and I will make you some dinner."

When he had finished eating, the giant set a white hen on the table. "Lay!" commanded the giant. And the hen laid a golden egg. "Lay!" repeated the giant, and the hen lay another golden egg.

Jack was amazed and his heart beat faster.

Jack hid patiently until the giant had fallen asleep. Then he scurried out of the oven, grabbed the hen, and ran out the door.

The hen started to squawk, which woke the giant. "Stop, thief!" he shouted, but Jack was already climbing down the beanstalk.

Jack and his mother were rich! Whenever they needed anything, Jack would tell the hen to lay another golden egg. And so they lived comfortably for some time.

Then one day, Jack's mother fell ill. The doctor could find no cure, and she grew weaker and sadder day by day. Jack tried to cheer her up, but nothing worked. "All the golden eggs in the world won't help," he said. Finally he decided to return to the giant's castle and see if he could find something there to lift his mother's sorrow.

Jack gathered all his courage and climbed up the beanstalk once more. This time when he entered the castle he hid inside a large pot.

"Fee-fi-fo-fum! I smell the blood of a little one!" roared the giant, and before his wife could reply, he went to the oven, but found nothing inside.

After dinner, the giant took out his magic harp. The harp played the most beautiful music Jack had ever heard—melodies so sweet and lilting that all who heard them were filled with joy.

The giant soon fell asleep, snoring loudly. Jack quietly lifted the lid off the pot and climbed out. But just as he reached for the harp, it began to scream, "Master! Master! A thief!" The giant woke to see Jack racing out the door. The giant seized a huge oak tree that he used as a club and went racing after Jack, shouting, "When I catch you, I'll eat you whole!"

Terrified, Jack ran as fast as he could, the giant following close behind, swinging his massive club. Jack reached the beanstalk and started down. The giant followed. His tremendous weight shook the beanstalk, making it sway to and fro.

When Jack reached the ground, the giant was nearly halfway down the beanstalk. "Bring me the axe!" he called to his mother, who fetched it as quickly as she could.

The giant climbed closer and closer. Jack swung the axe with all his might, chopping at the base of the beanstalk until it fell with a great crash, taking the giant with it over the mountainside. All that Jack could see of the giant was a single red boot nestled in a treetop far below.

No one ever knew what happened to the giant and his wife. As for Jack, the magic harp cured his mother's sadness with its beautiful music, and the magic hen kept laying golden eggs for them. The magic beans did indeed bring Jack and his mother great fortune—wealth and, more important, health and happiness ever after.

Library of Congress Cataloging-in-Publication Data is available.

This edition prepared by Cheshire Studio.

Trade edition

ISBN-10: 1-933327-11-1

ISBN-13: 978-1-933327-11-2

1 3 5 7 9 TE 10 8 6 4 2

Library edition

ISBN-10: 1-933327-12-X

ISBN-13: 978-1-933327-12-9

1 3 5 7 9 LE 10 8 6 4 2

Printed in Taiwan